# A WOLF
# & HIS WITCH

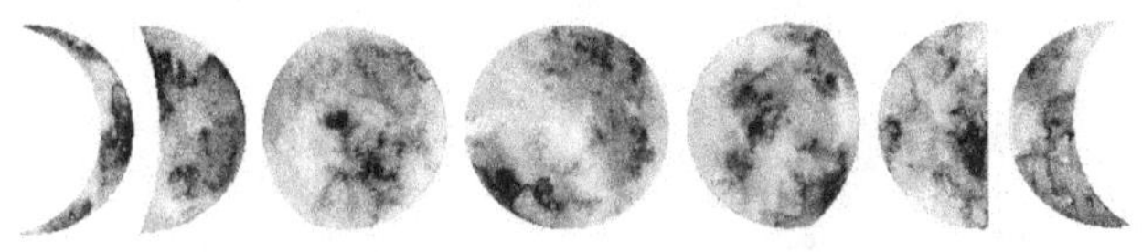

Z. BELLE

**Z. Belle**
**Ontario, Canada**
www.ourladyoflustandgrace.com



Author's Note: This is a work of fiction. Locales and public names are sometimes used for atmospheric purposes. Any resemblance to actual people, living or dead, or to businesses, companies, events, institutions, or locales are completely coincidental.

**A Wolf & His Witch/**
**Z. Belle 1st Edition**
ISBN 978-1-7771344-0-2

For my Wolf,

you are my muse, my twin flame

and my whole heart.

I love you.

(and Good Karen helped too, thanks mama.)

4

# ABOUT THE SERIES

*Three things cannot be long hidden:*
*The sun, the moon, and the truth*
*Buddha*

With *The Wolf & His Witch*, Z Belle brings you the first look at a new series that will leave you gasping and begging for more.

The Wolf & His Witch is the first in a series chronicling the powerful and carnal dichotomy between two twin flames, born and reborn as beasts and outcasts in this mortal realm.

Lifetimes spent lusting in ways they can never satisfy until they are reunited over and over again. This time as a wolf and a witch. Finally reconciling the struggle of being misunderstood and caged by the world, freeing each other from the bonds of humanity, finding sanctuary and exploring their true nature with restraints of their own design.

"The first time I saw your eyes all I could think was **Mine**. Like they had belonged to me and someone had stolen you from me. Then an overwhelming relief that I finally found you again." – Wolf

# WOLF

Something was wrong.

He was barely awake, not even sure why he was awake at all really. There was a low-grade panic gnawing at his stomach. He squinted in half sleep; eyes surveyed the room as he started the process of ascertaining whether there was a real threat looming or if he was still dreaming.

It was dark. She was curled up away from him in the wreck of their bed.

He could smell the remnants of soap on her skin. Felt her body heat. She was taking tiny inhales from her vape.

'Okay. We're both awake.'

Now to figure out why.

His innate nature dictated he was on high alert always, tenfold when she was with him. In this particular moment, he was no different.  Upon first glance, he saw nothing out of the ordinary. A dim light from the city filtered through the glass, this was ample for him to see everything in minute detail. The curtains danced lazily in the light breeze. He had left the sliding patio doors open so they could fall asleep listening to the thunderstorm. Her soaking wet sheets and discarded clothes lay in piles on the floor where they'd landed after a rather intense and playful fuck before bed. Likewise, a sizable vibrator still sat on the nightstand.  He didn't allow his eyes to linger on it too long, but his mouth curled up in the slightest grin thinking back on the activities of the evening prior.

Dog eared books and her laptop nestled among the clutter on her desk in one corner. His briefcase and work clothes laid neatly on the chair in the other. She had been so pleased with herself when she found it and dragged it home. It had been a perfect gift. Oversized, high backed monstrosity covered in rich, worn leather and so very comfortable. She had reverently dubbed it the 'Daddy' chair and knelt in front of him there often. She took better care of him and his things than her own and he adored her for this.

He breathed a sigh of relief, there was nothing physically wrong or out of place.

He couldn't hear anything unusual either, just the din of city traffic and her raspy shallow breathing. She'd been crying, recently even.

"What's wrong princess?"

She flinched a bit at the sound of his voice and his brow furrowed at this. He had not meant to startle her at all.

"I just had a bad dream Wolfy." Her voice was shaking and small. Seemed to come from far away. The tone of her voice and the nickname she'd chosen signaled she was feeling vulnerable, hovering near subspace. Usually his favorite of her moods, but this was different.

The arm he had casually slung over her in sleep tightened around her waist. She intertwined his fingers with hers, gripped them tight and pulled him closer, almost to the point of discomfort. But he didn't mind. He felt her attempting to meter her breathing and he automatically followed suit.

He was fully awake now and acutely aware of every miniscule movement she made. He could feel her rabbit heart beating hard against his forearm, she was scared. He moved closer to her, tucking himself in behind her so as much of his skin was touching hers as possible. She relaxed a little and wiggled closer for comfort. He felt the familiar rush of blood coursing towards his groin.

*Fuck.*

He wrestled trying to regain some control over his very primal, but understandable urges. His precious little witch. Soft, warm, small and currently quivering, curled into him. Under normal circumstances this was a vignette of perfect peacefulness for him, as well as an open invitation. But she was still visibly upset and withdrawn. He was vexed.

His eyes were fully capable of seeing in the low light and it wasn't helping. He gazed hungrily at the delicious curve of her back, the places she liked to be gripped hard and bitten. She was curled up on her side, one leg straight, the other bent knee touching her elbow. Her ass peeked out from under the sheets, turned towards him, begging to be grabbed and plundered again.

Her tattooed arm strewn over a pillow, fingers gripping the fabric of the pillowcase. He'd watched her in this position a hundred times, usually when he was fucking her from behind and she was about to cum. Her hands were always reaching and grasping even when tied. Dark hair that he had washed and brushed hours ago, framing her face. Bottom lip quivering as she fought back tears.

He shook his head trying to clear his thoughts and keep himself from taking her.

"I'm right here my love. It's alright."

He waited for her to tell him what she needed. As much as he wanted to fuck the monsters out of her, *right fucking now*, he would do whatever she asked of him. Even if it meant lying awake and standing guard, while he listened to her work through her dreams until she could fall back asleep. She was his, he protected her, always. His carnal needs could wait until morning.

He kissed her shoulder gently. The gesture meant to be nothing more than comforting, but she reacted instantly and favorably, twisting her neck and baring her throat in invitation. Her hand reached up and grabbed a fistful of his hair guiding his face towards her. Maddening mewling noises escaped her mouth. He followed her implied instructions and nibbled at her neck, fighting the urge to sink his teeth into her soft, yielding flesh. She sighed heavily and showed the barest hint of a smile, eyes still wet with tears. He kissed a tear from her cheek and growled a bit in spite of himself. Her reaction was instantaneous, she pushed her ass back into him and arched her back. He smiled, gripped her hipbone for leverage and murmured low and gruff into her ear.

"What do you need baby girl? Use your words." Anticipating more pouty noises and wiggling but she surprised him, she rolled over to face him, put her hand to his cheek and met his gaze.

She paused, took a deep breath and simply said, "Fuck me...hard." The first 2 words a whisper, the last, a command, quickly punctuated with a playful kiss. She added a very kitteny "please daddy." Sending him over the edge.

Before he could respond she disengaged her body from his and stretched herself out next to him. Back arched, hands above her head already crossed at the wrists, presenting herself to be held together and torn apart. She crossed her legs demurely in a blatantly bratty gesture. He welcomed the challenge, but first he was going to tease her until she submitted completely.

He was on top of her in an instant. His cock impossibly hard. He reached up, fingers closing around both of her wrists with room to spare. The other touched her face, she turned and kissed his palm, took one of his fingers into his mouth, cooing and sucking sweetly. He ran his hand slowly down the length of her torso, as slowly as he could manage. She usually loved being teased. But not now, she arched her back again, pushing her hips towards his fingers and squealing a protest.

"Want.

You.

Now."

Her voice quivering, guttural and punctuated by breathy moans.

"This Princess?" he gently parted her lips and touched her little clit with the slightest bit of pressure. She responded by bucking her hips up and squealing an agreement, almost managing to maneuver his fingers inside of her, she was very wet and waiting very impatiently.

"Not yet baby".

Princess pout.

"Mmmmmmore, pleeeeeease."

He pulled her legs apart, she moaned and spread them further in acquiescence. He positioned his hip on the inside of her thigh, managing to pin one leg, suddenly wishing he was an octopus instead so he could pin her and touch her everywhere all at once. Had they been in the playroom there were cuffs and ropes to keep her where he wanted, but they were in this bed and this was spontaneous. Necessary. Now. His eyes scanned the dimly lit room and fell upon a scarf she had worn to dinner on the floor, just out of reach.

He let go of her and attempted to get out of bed, she panicked and wrapped herself around him like a baby spider monkey, positioning her pussy so it tickled the tip of his cock and tried to maneuver herself onto him. He held her still with some difficulty, he sometimes forgot how strong she was. He kissed her forehead and she relaxed the slightest bit.

"One second baby".

She let go reluctantly and he eased her gently back down onto the bed.  Still pouting, she sat up, tucking her knees to her chest, wide eyed and watching. Shoulders only relaxing as she watched him walk back towards the bed.

He sat down next to her. She stayed in the same position but put her hands in front of her, wrists turned up and waiting for him to restrain her.

He was temporarily struck by the minutiae of this small moment.

Her trust, her vulnerability and their compatibility were absolute. They did everything to please each other, effortlessly it seemed. He fumbled with a slip knot, managed to tighten it just enough. Most of their bondage was implied. She could wiggle and will herself out of most every rope or knot he bound her with. She chose not to, willingly submitting to him, always. He lifted her hands over her head and laid her back down on the bed.

One look at her, stretched out, vulnerable, still shaking with the remnants of her dream and equal parts anticipation was enough to flip his internal switch from protector to predator, he was a hunter and he was suddenly terribly hungry for fresh rabbit heart. She looked up at him and smiled encouragement.

He forced her legs apart in one rough motion. Bent down and gave her pussy one incredibly wet lick, his broad tongue tracing a path upwards towards her neck as he raised up and plunged into her with a triumphant growl. He watched all the anxiety disappear from her brow as she cried out. Her breathy moans coming in sync with his rhythm. Self-control became excruciatingly difficult. She was so swollen almost closed, so warm, so wet, so perfect. But he wanted her shaking and thrashing uncontrollably underneath him. She always came first. And second and third and 22nd. He slowed down, entering her with deliberate, shallow strokes, coaxing her open. He had her legs pinned wide apart, but she still managed to wiggle her pussy underneath him in an attempt to take more than what he was giving. He reacted by just holding her down harder, moving ever so carefully, waiting. Patiently waiting to be rewarded.

As if on cue, the softest, guttural moans escaped her throat. Lips pursing and parting. Groans begat whimpers. He started to pause between strokes. All her muscles turned from yielding to rigid. He could feel her pussy contracting around his cock, trying to hold him in place or draw him in further. But he wasn't ready to give in just yet. She had admitted to him more than once that she loved this part of the tease and he reveled in it.

Once more. A little deeper. A longer pause. And again, rough this time, he completely buried himself in her. Her pussy pulsed hard almost pushing him out, she squealed and thrashed her head back and forth.

"Pleeeeeease Daddy. PLEEEEEEASE."

He needed no further encouragement. He drew back until he was barely touching her slick opening. With one fluid motion he buried himself to the hilt in her convulsing and suddenly gushing wet pussy. He fucked her hard and deep.  Sprays of liquid splashing up both their torsos. She screamed and cried out incoherently as though speaking in tongues. Her eyes rolled back showing the whites in complete surrender. Her thrashing slowed. Her body seemed to melt under his.

He let go of his death grip on her thighs and wrapped his arms around her waist pulling her closer. She hooked her legs around his hips and drew him deeper. He reached up quickly and pulled the knot from her makeshift bondage. She immediately put her hands around his neck and pressed her forehead to his. Moving in perfect unison, he felt her hips tilting and accommodating as much of his monstrous cock as she could.  He felt her frantically rubbing her clit against his pubic bone. He slowed again and pushed his cock as far as she could take. She let out a scream and her body stiffened as she held him impossibly close. He felt another orgasm surge through her body and wash over them both like waves. She fell back into the pillows. Her eyelashes fluttering showing the whites of her eyes, her lips moving murmuring nonsensically. He was close to breaching himself but wanted to push her even farther over the edge if possible.

He repeated his slow, deliberate movements until she regained some semblance of lucidity. Slid one hand up her body, cupping her breast before gently closing around her throat. She arched her back again, straining towards him.

"No no nononononono". The edges of her lips curled up into a half smile around the protests that meant "absolutely yes". He could feel another of her impending orgasms building with his. Deeper now. Her voice sounded panicked, but he knew she was ready to slip over the edge, as was he. He couldn't control himself any longer.  He could hear her cries and his own growling disconnected as though they were coming from another room.

He managed to get out the words "where do you want me to cum".

"Inside me.  Fill me." Her voice cracked; she was close to tears.

One final, triumphant roar and he did as she'd asked. Every primal instinct to mark her and claim her as his own satisfied at her request. Her legs tightened around his waist, his cock and her pussy exploding in union. A shockwave rolled through them both. Followed by the low rumble of an earthquake.

She pulled his entire body weight down on top of her. He knew she wasn't ready to let go. His orgasm slowly dissipated, and he found himself returning to reality and enjoying the sensation of her quivering and shaking underneath him. Her pussy still twitching and milking his cock with the aftershocks of their last orgasm.

He only disengaged and rolled slightly to the side when he felt her starting to cry. He was met with another whimper of protest. Slightly saucy now. Princess pout.

He recalled the first time she had cried after he had fucked her, way back when they had first met and were still exploring each other. She'd curled into a ball on the bed, covering her face with her hands and tried to hide it from him. He did now what he'd done then. Kissed her forehead, kissed her cheek and pulled her closer to him.

"Was that good baby?"

"Mmmhmm." She nodded. Staring straight through him with sparkling panda eyes.

"Did that make you feel better?"

An emphatic "mmmmhmmm" and a tiny giggle.

He'd taken her from a bad dream to good subspace. And now he needed a shower. Desperately. They both did.
She didn't protest when he got up this time and followed him shortly after on shaking legs.

Nothing could compare to the sex they had. He'd never experienced anything like it. The way their bodies fit together, how she encouraged him effortlessly with every whimper and small movement. How she was able to accommodate every inch of him and still somehow wordlessly beg for more. Whether it was quick and playful easy Sunday morning sex or intense bondage sessions that stretched on for hours of toys, teasing and play. Or what they had just done, purely passionate and spontaneous in the middle of the night. But he had to admit showering with her and holding her afterwards held a close second.

She embraced both sides of him equally and completely. The rough, bestial, conquering wolf side and his stoic desires to protect and care for her. She was a strong, intelligent, capable woman, the most independent woman he had ever met. But she had chosen to give herself over to him completely and this was pure bliss. Her legs were still trembling, he held her with a firm grip around the waist while his other hand washed the remnants of what they had just done off her skin. When she started getting extra sooky he turned off the water, wrapped her in a towel and held her close before carrying her back to bed.

When they were both decontaminated, he tucked her into clean sheets and then into him. He waited for her to drift back to sleep and soon followed.

# WITCH 

Something was wrong.

It was terribly dark, almost pitch black. She had to deliberately blink a few times to make sure her eyes were actually open, and she could still barely see at all. The air felt incredibly thick and heavy, to the point where her breathing felt labored, a claustrophobic feeling adding to her already growing panic. It was ungodly hot, she felt sticky and sweaty but somehow still had goosebumps. Her skin was crawling. She felt the unpleasant shocks of panic shooting through her muscles, but she wasn't awake enough to ascertain why. She didn't even really know where she was.

She felt a familiar sensation of rope biting into her flesh and realized she had woken up in a hammock. This was definitely not Kansas, and this was not her apartment. She could hear jungle noises, cicadas trilled, and the patter of soft rain, rustling leaves, unknown creatures calling out to each other in the night. A twig snapped sharp against the din, then everything went horribly quiet.

A bolt of terror shot through her as she realized she wasn't alone. Someone (or something) was creeping around outside of this primitive hut she had woken up in. She felt hunted and not in the exhilarating way she was used to with her Wolf. As her eyes slowly adjusted to the absence of light, she saw hurricane shutters over windows set into thatched walls and a flimsy looking door. These were the only barriers between her and whatever was outside.

She moved her body slowly into a seated position and put her feet down, carefully as not to make any noise, wincing at the creak of the ropes as she rose. Grateful for the silence provided by the dirt floor as she padded deliberately towards the shutters to close them. She sighed ever so slightly when she saw hook and eye latches, she circled around the inside of the hut and painstakingly locked each one.

She froze and stifled a scream as she saw fingers reaching through slats beside the door. A masculine hand fumbling around trying to find a way in.

"I know you're in there, I'm coming for you." An aggressive male voice with a slight southern twang. Not Texas...Alabama maybe? her panic grew as she ascertained that absolutely nothing was making any sense at all.

She pressed her back against the door and tried desperately to hold her breath. Adrenalin coursed through her veins sending electric shocks through her entire nervous system.

"He'll never find you." The threatening voice now sounded familiar, but in her current state she couldn't place it.

Her eyes darted around the room. Not only did she have no idea where she was, or what was happening, but where was her Wolf? She was completely alone, and the place was completely empty save the hammock and a broken chair. The only exit blocked. No Wolf, no weapons, no escape. Trapped in a flimsy cage in god's good nowhere apparently. Her panic took full hold, screeching obscenities in her head. *He left you, he never wanted you, you deserve this.* Suddenly the man's voice outside mimicked her inner thoughts in a mocking tone reminiscent of the wicked witch of the west, horrible thoughts and words overlapping until she about went mad.

She risked a peek through the pried open shutter. Her tormentor was the bad guy from a movie she had watched 100 times.

She had one crystal clear, somewhat calming thought.

'Okay, this is obviously a dream, I just need to wake up.' She exhaled slowly, closed her eyes and willed herself to do just that.

Her relief was short lived. His hand reached through the opening and grabbed her arm in a vice like grip, she couldn't contain her screams. The only muscles working were her vocal cords, she was otherwise completely paralyzed with fear. Everything felt like stop motion, the room suddenly lit up with a sickly yellow strobe light that couldn't decide if it wanted to flash quickly or slow. She felt sick and disoriented.

She closed her eyes again, trying to will herself to wake up and she felt an arm around her waist, gently pulling her aside.

"Here, just hold it closed and I will lock it."
It was one of her girlfriends from back home, suddenly appearing out of thin air.

She did as she was told and as she put her hands on the door, it changed. No longer rustic and weak, it metamorphosized into her apartment door. Her friend turned the lock on the deadbolt and affixed the chain in place and said, "it's okay. We can just wait here 'til he gets back." She allowed herself to be led over to the bed, laid down and closed her eyes.

And with that, she woke up.

The worst of her nightmares always ended with her climbing back into her bed. Made it almost impossible to separate the strands of the dream still tangled with reality. Her heart felt like it was about to explode from her chest and that horrible hysteria hovered close by, threatening to take over again. She forced herself to stay still. Her breathing was rapid and shallow, she felt close to hyperventilating. She could hear the heavy breathing of her Wolf asleep behind her and this calmed her just the slightest bit. She focused and tried to match the cadence of the air entering and exiting her lungs with his but was failing miserably.

She'd pulled her body away from his in her sleep and was currently curled into a tight ball. She focused her concentration on the only point of contact between them, the intense heat of his hand holding her around the waist, still willing herself to calm the fuck down. Her muscles refused to relax completely, still half frozen, stuck between fight or flight. Her eyes continued to dart around the room, wanting to make sure she was truly awake this time, but she saw monsters in every corner and shadow.

She focused on small vignettes of the day and night before and the memories began to pull her back from her hysteria. Reassuring herself that was not a pile of writhing snakes on the rug, but her dress still wet from getting caught in the warm, evening rain in a puddle on the floor. He had undressed her carefully at first, then torn a strap when she got stuck, he had been overly eager to free her from her clothes. Likewise, that was not a crouching monster ready to pounce, but a pile of bedding she had soaked through at the mercy of his talented fingers and tongue, tossed aside carelessly, waiting to be washed.

She had more sets of sheets in the linen closet than she did pots and pans in the cupboard. She had to. He coaxed rivers from her pussy every time they were together without fail. Last night was no different, and tomorrow would hopefully be the same. He would kiss her goodbye; she would get up and put the apartment back to right so they could ruin it again when he got home.

The massive, leather, 'Daddy' chair in one corner was not an angry troll. Simply a comfortable throne for a humble king. His clothes were already laid out over the back for the next morning. This was a sweet but selfish ritual, she knew if he didn't have to rush around in the morning, they could spend a few extra minutes in bed together. His briefcase was packed, and the coffee pot filled, timer set to 5 minutes before his alarm. She loved waking up next to him and their stolen moments sipping coffee and holding each other in the morning.

Her desk was how she'd left it. The exact opposite. Chaos to his order. 3 half read books piled next to her laptop covering scribbled on scraps of paper and bar napkins with cryptic notes. The speaker light flashed, beckoning. She wanted to get up and put music on, and would have had she been alone, every lamp and light in the room too at this point. The darkness was his territory, she was a creature of the light. She was wide awake and still shaken. The rain had stopped, and the city was audible again. A dog barked in the distance, light traffic noises and a siren far away.

As badly as she wanted to get up, check the locks on the door, turn the lights on and escape the horrors of the nightmare she'd had, she refused to get out of bed or move much at all, she didn't want to wake him. But...she needed nicotine in a way that could no longer be denied and tentatively reached a hand towards the nightstand, almost knocking a carelessly placed sex toy to the floor. Whoops. She smiled briefly thinking on the night before, but her dream came flooding back. Someone had wanted to take her away from Him, she panicked all over again at the memory. A mantra of 'I can't go back' started looping in her head and she gripped her vape pen in one hand and the pillow in the other and pulled it towards her face, trying to stifle her sobs.

"What's wrong princess?" she jumped at the sound of his voice.

'Fuck, I woke him up.' She thought and chastised herself.

She managed to whisper the words "I just had a bad dream Wolfy." Trying to keep the panic out of her voice and failing miserably. What she really wanted was to pry open his chest and crawl inside so she could feel safe, awaken the beast so she would feel safe or at least have him hold her painfully tight until she could shake the creeping tendrils of that horrible dream. But she was already vexed that she had woken him at all. His sleep was precious, even more so when the moon was waxing in the night sky.

He read her mind and pulled her close. She took the opportunity, twined her tiny fingers into his and pulled his hand to her chest. His forearm grazed her nipple ever so slightly and tingled under his touch. She found this arousing and soothing and was finally able to get her breathing under some semblance of control. She realized he was breathing deep and deliberately trying to help her. It worked. She wiggled back into him instinctively and felt his cock stiffened ever so slightly against the small of her back. Her inner brat insisted she wiggle just a little bit more. She fought the urge and failed miserably, which brought a fresh batch of tears to the corner of her eyes. Her body hitched with a fresh sob.

"I'm right here my love, it's alright." His authoritative tone was always calming. She melted into him a little bit more and waited to see if he would fall back asleep.

She really didn't want to lay awake while he slept, she wanted him to rip her apart and hold her together in the way only he could. Had it been any other time she would have just asked him to fuck her, but neither one of them had planned on being awake at 3am, and he had to get up for work in a few hours.

Blissfully, he kissed her shoulder, with the barest hint of a playful nibble and her body reacted on its own. She instinctively bared her throat. Encouraging whimpers escaped from her mouth. She reached up and tangled her fingers in his hair pulling him closer, in case he changed his mind.

He didn't.

He kissed and bit her neck gently. She smiled as he licked the salt from her face. She had never met a man who had much more than tolerated her habit of crying at every little thing (good or bad or overwhelming), much less encouraged it and loved it as he did. He saw her tears as tangible proof that he had pleased her, it was the absolute truth. She felt her contentment return. Her hips undulated in slow circles, she pressed herself up against him to telegraph her want.

"What do you need baby girl? Use your words." His voice was a perfect blend of playful and commanding and left no question in her mind that he wanted her, right fucking now.

She flipped over in one fluid motion and faced him, lost for a minute in his perfect mouth, the corners pulled up in a playful grin exposing insanely sharp, blinding white canines. She touched his beard to once again reassure herself that he was real, and this was really happening. Felt herself drowning in his beautiful dark eyes. She took a deep breath to center herself and simply said "Fuck me…hard." The last word felt like it was channeled from somewhere else. Not submissive *at all*. She was not in the habit of issuing orders, so she padded it quickly with a kiss and a "please Daddy."

He didn't seem to object. Her earlier stress had almost completely dissipated, she felt her muscles relaxing as she stretched out next to him and presented herself for his pleasure.

He took immediate advantage of her prone position. His huge hand gripping her tiny wrists. She couldn't move if she had wanted to. She didn't want to. He caressed her face sending shivers through her entire body. She kissed his palm and sucked his finger barely aware of the noises she was making. Her entire body felt like molten metal, every heart beat a rush of heat and noise. Tendrils of electricity reaching out of her core rushing to meet anywhere his fingers touched. Her pussy was screaming arias, wanting to be fondled and filled.

He traced his fingertip down the center of her torso, she bucked and squealed trying to get him to where she wanted. Heard her own voice as if someone else was grunting through her mouth,

**Want.**

**You.**

**Now.**

"This princess?" he barely touched her clit and an electrical surge shot through her body, her hips moved of their own accord, she felt the tips of his fingers tickle her opening and she maneuvered her hips as much as she could and tried to get them inside.

Denied.

"Not yet baby." Her bottom lip jutted out; her eyes huge, ready to spill tears at any second. He called it her princess pout. It usually worked to get her what she wanted but he was being stubborn.

'Okay, maybe it worked', she thought as he deftly pinned one leg underneath his thigh with the perfect amount of pressure. His huge paw of a hand closed around the inside of her other thigh and pried her legs wide apart. She didn't fight this at all. She relaxed and readied herself for whatever he was about to do next.

*Wait*

*What?*

*Noooooo*

*Not this*

He let go of her and tried to lift himself up. *No, no, no* (panic). She immediately wrapped herself around him and held on for dear life. He reassured her and gently pried her arms from around his neck. She acquiesced reluctantly and let go, allowing herself to be lowered back onto the bed. She sat up to see where he was going. Bathroom? Playroom? Toy box? Away?

'*Don't leeeeeeeeeeeave,*' the voice in her head became a keen wailing sound.

She felt a bit ridiculous for overreacting when she realized he was just grabbing something to tie her up with. She turned her wrists up and waited. He sat down in front of her on the bed and started to bind her hands with one of her scarves. He stopped suddenly, for a moment it felt like he was staring right through her. She was overcome with love for him in that moment. The trust she had for him was overwhelming. It scared her sometimes. There was nothing she wouldn't do with him and for him. She belonged to him in every way.

The feel of the fabric tightened around her wrists brought her submissive comfort. She knew he would stay and play with her until she was sated and undone, and he would put her back together when they were finished satisfying each other. She felt an exquisite combination of small and vulnerable, and at the same time ferociously protected and more than a little bit hunted. He was the perfect dominant. She had always struggled to submit in the time called before, wanting to but never finding anyone worthy; until him. They had slipped into their roles seamlessly from the very beginning, as if it was always meant to be that way. She had long felt that she never really had a choice when it came to loving him, belonging to him and that realization had never bothered at all.

She knew she would have loved him just as much had he been less beautiful or not so well endowed. He was the most amazing, intelligent, complicated creature she had ever encountered in all her days. But as fate had allowed, he was her perfect match in every way. He was so beautiful. Chiseled jaw accentuated by a silky, well-manicured beard.

Wicked smile and sharp canines behind delicious lips. His smile was one of her favorite things on earth. His freckled tanned skin covered in sigil tattoos. Thick shock of black curls, perfect for running her fingers through. Dark eyes she drowned in, that became golden prisms in the sunlight. He was exactly the right height for her tall frame, her head rested in that perfect spot on his chest and all she had to do was tilt her head up the slightest bit to be rewarded with forehead kisses. They made a beautiful couple.

And the sex was unparalleled. His sexual prowess and stamina were incredible. Unprecedented. She found herself in constant shock, awe and bliss when he was fucking her. Half the time her body was so overwhelmed she didn't know how to respond. She learned very early on to stop fighting it and just let go.

He was her perfect partner.

His incredibly huge cock was reminiscent of her darkest hentai fantasies and filled her up to the breaking point and then some. His perfect curve matching hers, they fit like puzzle pieces.

She came back to reality briefly as he lifted her arms up over her head and gently laid her back down on the bed, assuming their previous positioning. She watched his face change in front of her eyes, her favorite moment, this magnificent transformation from man to monster. She smiled up at him, welcoming the transition. Her Wolf, her beast. She would take everything he gave her and beg for more. Her body quivered in anticipation and she was soon rewarded.

She felt him spread her legs and she forced herself apart even wider until her lower half resembled a wishbone, trembling at the breaking point. He lifted his body up, briefly away from her and swooped down in one fluid motion, she felt his wide, wet tongue part her pussy lips and add to her impossible wetness. Her synapses firing rapidly as sparks lit up under her skin following the trail his tongue made. That was nothing compared to the moment he entered her.

The fireworks started slowly building in her belly. The stop motion sensation returning from her dream, but this time it was bliss. She fought to keep her eyes open in the overwhelm so she could look at him. She was quickly losing control of everything, including her voice, crying out every time he thrust into her. She couldn't help it. Her thoughts became unintelligible noises and sensations. He had given her this exquisite gift of feeling safe enough to completely let go and she gladly surrendered to this, and him.

She felt him slow down, she rocked her hips back and forth as much as she could to accommodate as much as he was willing to give. She tried to take a little more. He was having none of this, he pinned her harder and she submitted immediately. She felt an orgasm slowly gaining strength like a small hurricane in her core. She was in the eye of it now, complete calm, the only sound their synchronized breathing and a distant roar getting closer by the second. She knew this one was going to be huge and fought to keep from bracing herself, allowing herself to be swept up in the moment. Quite like staring at the ocean on a seemingly calm day to see a tsunami approaching shore, if she could stand her ground it would engulf her and carry her away.

He was growling with the effort of controlling himself. He was a wolf and she wanted all of him, raw and untamed carnal violence. Right. Now.

"Pleeeeeeeease Daddy. PLEEEEEEASE."

He pulled almost all the way out, her pussy protested this, and she felt her muscles spasm trying to draw him back inside. With one rough motion she was sated. He entered her fully, completely burying himself in her over and over, snarling and growling.

So much pleasure and not nearly enough words for it. Rocket launches and Aurora Borealis on the 4th of July. Hurricanes and tidal waves. And lightning. All the lightning.

Then nothing.

Blissful floating nothing.

She re-emerged from delicious darkness and back into the moment. He was playing her body perfectly. He shot her a wicked toothsome grin; he knew exactly what he was doing...exactly what she needed. The maddening tease, the build-up before he carried her into subspace. She savored every movement, every stroke, every look, every growl and breath.

With one deft movement he plunged deep into her, she felt her body respond immediately, pulsing sensations radiating out from the walls of her pussy through every part of her body and even into the air around them.

Perfect union.

Her last tangible thought before she slipped over the edge. The closest she had come to describing it was falling, but on the moon, into clouds. A slow decent with the softest landing, surrounded by darkness, complete silence and utter peacefulness.

She melted beneath him.

Time didn't exist in this place. Nor pain, nor clear thoughts of any kind, just wave after wave of warmth and pleasure.

She slowly regained consciousness. She could hear the wetness of her pussy ejaculating before the rest of her senses caught up and she felt a luxurious slippery sensation where his body met hers. He was pleased with himself, grinning and growling with every movement now, she knew the best was about to come.

She felt his hands leave her thighs, and her hands freed from bondage, she wrapped herself around him without breaking their conjoined rhythm. Slow now, like lazy ripples on a pond. Everywhere his hands touched sending sparks through her skin, she felt his fingers close around her throat and strained towards him, unable to articulate her pleasure. It came out sounding more like 'nonononono', which everyone knows is sub speak for 'more more more'. He told her she spoke in tongues when she was about to cum and she believed him.

She was close again, and now so was he, she could feel it coming off him in waves. Deeper now, but not all the way. Lucidity slipping away with every stroke.

She heard his voice and pulled herself back from the brink.

"Inside me. Fill me up." The words crackling with the pressure on her throat, coming out as demanding and guttural. His voice roared and echoed in her ears and she held onto him for dear life. They came in unison, bodies reacting to each other with exquisite synchronicity.

No matter how many times this happened, it always felt impossibly perfect.

Spectacular.

She was shaking uncontrollably under him and pulled his full body weight down on top of her trying to quell the spasming in seemingly every muscle in her body. She loved these moments, right after, fully aware of every cell in her body, the pain, the pleasure. Almost too much to bear but she wouldn't trade this for anything.

She could feel her pussy quivering around his cock even after the rest of her body had relaxed.

Everything hit her all at once and she knew she was going to cry. Happy, overwhelmed submissive tears this time. She fought her long-ingrained instinct to hide her face, instead just letting the overwhelm wash over her. He rolled off to the side, so he was facing her, still with a protective arm around her waist. His beard tickled her face and he tasted ever tear as it fell. He kissed her forehead and she began to compose herself, slowly, taking her time. They snuggled into each other in the wreck of the bed, neither one wanting to get up just yet.

"Was that good baby?"

He always asked, as if he wasn't holding a puddle of a girl in his arms. Wet everywhere, aftershocks still hitting her intermittently and making her shake.

She looked up at him, smiling huge. "Mmmmhmmmm."

She was always afraid to talk too much right after, still feeling the effects of subspace and did not want to sound clingy and mildly insane. She felt a lot of both in this moment.

"Did that make you feel better?"

She nodded and giggled a bit. "Mmmmmhmmmm."

Her bad dreams completely forgotten she realized they were both covered in sweat and ejaculate, the breeze coming in the window raising goosebumps on her damp skin. She shivered as he got out of bed. Watched him in awe as he crossed the room and closed the patio door, his immense frame silhouetted against the city lights outside. She waited until she heard the shower running and sat up. Bambi legs still shaking, she leaned heavily on the bed for balance as she pulled the sheets off, replacing them with a set that was clean and dry. The duvet had slipped off in the melee and was salvageable for another night.

As soon as that was done, she joined him in the shower. Surrendering to the ritual of being tenderly washed and dried off before they returned to bed. As rough as he was when they were fucking, he was an exquisite juxtaposition of incredibly gentle and kind afterwards, always doting on her and making her feel safe and loved, and exceptionally clean. She focused her thoughts on the more pleasant events of the day before as he wrapped her up in a towel and carried her to bed. She felt protected and perfectly sore and drifted off quite peacefully tucked perfectly into him.

# WOLF

It was exceptionally warm for a late December afternoon, it had been an arduously long, hot day. The air was thick and heavy. So was traffic for that matter. His bones were warning of a storm coming but the temperature still hadn't plummeted when the sun went down and there was not even a hint of a tell-tale breeze. The sky was turning pink as he rode home, making it feel later than it was adding to his growing frustration. He should have been home by now.

The good weather meant he'd been able to take his Harley to work at least. Riding usually helped him decompress after a shit day at the office, but today he felt rushed, he was not enjoying the commute at all. He just wanted to be home and was grateful for the ability to weave in and out of traffic. The office had been the same. Maneuvering around one unpleasant task and onto the next, one exercise in patience after another. Hours felt like days. Truth be told, from the minute he'd locked the door behind him that morning all he could think about was getting back to her. The urgency to be with her only getting stronger as he got closer. He heard her siren song loud and clear, calling him home.

He could see her in his mind's eye. Flashes of white against her tanned skin. He reached for her and was rewarded with a smile; she was waiting for him. It was in these moments that he not so silently thanked and cursed the universe simultaneously. It was a maddening thing to be 40 years old and to only now begin to understand what real love was. How to give it and how to receive it. How to trust someone with every terrifying piece of what he was and still feel accepted fully and unequivocally. She knew every terrible thing he had ever done, everything he kept hidden from the world and still loved him with a patience and depth that didn't seem possible. He railed against the universe for gifting and cursing him as it had. Making him what he was and moreover making him wait so long to find her. But at the end of the day, he was grateful. Grateful to have her to return to. Finally feeling like 'happily ever after' was attainable.

He was forced out of his musings and back to reality by the obnoxious blast of a car horn. Lost in thought, he'd been sitting at a green light. Truth be told, he barely remembered exiting the highway. He thanked the gods as he found himself close to journey's end.  He was overheated, heavily distracted and weary. A few more blocks and an elevator ride were all that was keeping him from her now.

He perked his ears up and listened for music playing into the hallway as he approached her apartment. He smirked while he searched his pockets for his key, he could almost always tell what was waiting for him on the other side of the door by what she was playing. He amused himself with this game almost every day, he was rarely ever wrong.

Some days she was twisted up like a yogi in her desk chair, hair gathered in a mess on the top of her head stuck through with forgotten pencils. Typing or scribbling maniacally or staring intently whilst listening to an odd array of top 40 starlets and overly gentle sounding men with acoustic guitars. Those were the days he slipped in quietly, not wanting to break her concentration.

If she was cooking, cleaning or concocting potions, she was listening to oldies and always dropped whatever she was doing to hold him and kiss him. More often than not, he got too carried away with their reunions; plates and spells had been broken, and dinner had been burnt more than once while he bent her over the kitchen island and fucked her hello after a long day.

Instrumental anything meant and she was curled up on the couch reading. Absorbed in ancient texts and folklore somedays and others researching her main source of income, thumbing through a trashy romance novel, taking notes and sometimes playing with herself absentmindedly.

And any genre of music playing loud meant she was finished writing for the day, she was pleased with herself and watching porn on the big screen trying to hide the noises from the neighbors.

Those were his favorite days.

Meant she wanted to be caught, tied up, played with and punished.

And he was always happy to oblige.

He paused at the door and realized he didn't hear anything at all. Hmmm. Strange, he had felt her so clearly awake not that long ago. He rationalized perhaps she had fallen asleep waiting for him. He turned his key and opened the door quietly; he didn't want to wake her, thinking it would be a lovely respite after a long day to slip in bed next to her and just relax for a while.

His smile disappeared quickly as he surveyed the main room, his brow furrowing as he ascertained she wasn't anywhere to be seen.

Her apartment was their sanctuary. For all intents and purposes, it appeared to be a decent sized studio loft. One wall of windows with a small concrete balcony accessible by a set of patio doors.
Open concept kitchen separated from the main area by a simple island. Open concept everything really, her apartment consisted of one giant room. Sparsely decorated save the plants and herbs everywhere. On every surface, hanging from the ceiling, affixed to the walls, dried and stored in jars with her spidery handwriting labeling this or that. Like a little garden apothecary juxtaposed inside a concrete high rise. The living and sleeping space artfully separated from workspace just by the deliberate placement of furniture, a few gauzy curtains and yes, more plants.

The fading pink light of the sky illuminated the room. The bed was meticulously made and empty, she wasn't in it. The couch had been tidied, blankets folded, pillows straightened, but she wasn't on it. Her desk was likewise unoccupied. The light was on in the kitchen, dishes drying in the rack, coffee pot half full and still warm. There was a book and a mug on the coffee table. But she was nowhere to be seen.

He listened intently for the sound of water running, and heard nothing of the sort, she wasn't in the shower. He had the thought to check and see if he missed a text about her going out when he heard it. The faint sound of a heartbeat? Dah dum, dah dum. Not a heartbeat, drums. War drums at that. He dropped his things where he stood and strode across the living room.

They rarely had traditional guests. That being said, anyone just popping by or even staying a while would have no reason to think there might be anything behind that bookshelf.

But there was.

He slid it easily to one side along the wall and was greeted by the sight of her reclined on their other bed, fucking herself with a dildo to the rhythm of Viking war drums.

"Hello my Wolf." She stopped what she was doing and smiled sweetly. "Welcome home."

He stood smiling and seemingly transfixed in the doorway as his eyes scanned the room. The windows and 2 of the walls were covered in thick padding and heavy drapery to keep their chaos contained and the light out. The bed was a heavily modified four-poster monstrosity that took up the bulk of the space. The base had been reinforced against excessive activities. They had broken more than one bedframe before custom building this one. They had added tie off points, O-rings screwed into the base and posts at carefully calculated intervals. A simple yoga sling hung in one corner. The entire room reflected by a giant floor to ceiling mirror strategically placed. One remaining wall was completely covered in pegboard. Like a typical man would use in his garage to hold his tools. But he was not a typical man at all, and these were tools, but of a different sort. Straps and restraints, whips and ropes displayed beautifully and artfully, while still being within easy reach. There was an old steamer trunk at the end of the bed and a video camera on a nightstand in the other corner.

And her in the middle of the bed, wearing nothing but a white lace garter belt and a pair of sheer white stockings.

"What's my princess doing with my pussy?" he snarled playfully, channeling his inner big bad wolf perfectly.

"Getting ready for you." She stated very matter of factly. She was propped up on a wedge-shaped pillow and spread her legs just a little more so he could watch her pull the phallic rubber thing out of her perfect little pussy. His eyes caught the slightest little sparkle and he realized she was wearing her favorite princess plug. She really was getting ready for him. He growled deep in his throat.

She moved gracefully to the edge of the bed, assumed a demure kneeling position and patted the bed between her knees in an unnecessary invitation.

'Welcome home indeed', he thought to himself as he closed the space between them. The last 8 hours suddenly forgotten, everything forgotten, except for her, here and now. He held her face in both his hands and kissed her forehead, breathing her in. She always smelled like incense smoke and spice, like a temple somewhere exotic and far away.

He stood in front of her and she reverently unbuttoned his work shirt, unbuckled his belt and helped him out of his clothes. He pulled her towards his chest, undoing the bun from the top of her head and running his fingers through her insanely thick, long black hair. It smelled of bourbon and honey and felt like silk. She pressed the cool of her cheek onto the warmth of his torso before shimmying down a little and taking the tip of his cock into her mouth.

His inner dialog became guttural grunts and moans.

Want.

Her.

Now.

His fingers became fists in her hair, muscles flexing and straining as he guided his cock deeper and deeper into her throat. She took all of it until he felt her choke a bit, then a lot and he begrudgingly let her up for air. He looked down at her face as she licked the spit from her lips and gazed adoringly up at him with teary eyes and he realized he couldn't wait one more minute. He had to be inside her.

The dynamic between them was crystal clear to even the most casual of observers. She belonged to him, completely. They were the perfect example of a dominant and submissive couple. But every now and again she would pleasantly surprise him by very delicately dictating what she wanted. He never felt forced, only guided gently, and he loved it. This was one of those days. He knew she had something in mind, something she was craving, and he was happy to oblige. He already knew what it was, but he wanted to hear her say it.

He grabbed her firmly by the chin, tipped her head up and met her gaze. "Tell me what you want princess."

She squirmed a little and tried to drop her eyes. He wouldn't let her. "Say it baby girl, tell me what you want me to do to you."

"I want...I want..." she stammered and took a deep breath, "I want you to fuck me in the ass. Please." The last sentence tumbled out of her mouth in a rush, almost one as one word.

"Of course, my princess, but first, bend over and let me look at you." He smiled down at her with a rapacious grin.

She did as she was told, pausing only to position the pillow under her torso, pressed her chest to the bed and raised her hips to the perfect height. Her tattooed cheeks artfully framed by the lace of the garters, pussy lips just the slightest bit swollen and the crystal end of the princess plug sparkling in the light. He positioned himself behind her and enjoyed the view. One of those gorgeous moments that should have been photographed, but... princess wants, princess gets. She turned her head to the side and smiled back at him. She had expressed her desires and gracefully handed full control back to him. She was his to do with as he pleased. He rubbed the tip of his cock against her opening. She quivered and shook, arched her back even more inviting him in.

He entered her, slowly, enjoying the sensation of her pulsing warmth. As he pressed himself all the way in, she squealed and tried to push back into him. He reached forward and placed his hand firmly between her shoulder blades, rendering her immobile and continued his slow movements, matching his rhythm to the drums still playing in the background.

She acquiesced and low purring noise escaped her lips, she was thrumming and humming, the spasms of her pussy becoming more intense, "are you going to cum for me baby?"

"ohmygodyesimgonnacumimgonnacumimgonnacum ." Her voice cracked and she cried out as he picked up the tempo of his thrusts. Her entire body tensed under him, and then suddenly, with a whimper, she relaxed completely.

"Is that what you wanted my love?" he asked her as the effects of her orgasm dissipated.

"Yes Wolfy." She smiled and cooed over her shoulder, eyelashes still fluttering, breath coming in tiny wisps and pants.

He cocked his head to the side and spanked her, hard and open handed, more for shock value and noise than pain. It worked and she jumped and giggled. He thrust into her once more and she moaned, turning her face into the bed in an attempt to stifle a groan.

"Maybe you didn't hear me darling. I said, is that what you wanted?" he commanded quietly. Raising his hand, ready to spank her again.

She turned her head to the side and with a very shy smile said "yes," she flinched, "and No."

Instead of spanking her, he dropped his hand and caressed the red mark he'd left on her backside. "Good girl."

She reached back, gently pulled the plug, dropping it nonchalantly off the side of the bed where it landed with a metallic clank, its purpose had been served. With both hands she held herself open.

She simply said "Now you. Please."

He didn't need to be asked twice.

He squeezed a copious amount of lube onto the palm of his hand and slathered it over his already wet cock. He couldn't resist fingering her pussy a little bit as he coated her threshold with the rest, slowly moved his palm up and down between her legs until she shook, and she mewled with a lot of pleasure and little protest. She was taking very slow, deep breaths, he felt her tense, then relax and tense up again.

"It's okay baby, I won't hurt you." The beast inside him remained contained. This was not the time or place for carnal or rough. He simply waited for the right moment, firmly gliding his cock over where his hand had been until she had fully calmed herself. She squeaked and froze a little as he coaxed the tip barely inside, he was in perfect control, grinning down at his frightened little fae. He was incredibly happy in this moment; she was absolutely perfect.

He truly did not want to hurt her; his reward was her submission. He waited until she was ready, watching the most miniscule of movements, until she was no longer tensing, flinching and attempting to move away. He entered her with maddening care, stopping when her body communicated 'stop' and easing forward slowly when her face said 'go' and she had managed to relax again. This was part of the pleasure for him, her fear was obvious, palpable and intoxicating to him. To know that she was truly terrified, but she was still willing to trust him. It was a feeling like no other. Her ass was impossibly tight, it felt like time was moving in slow motion as was he. An exercise in trust and patience, he waited until her body gave into him. And it did, little by little then seemingly all at once.

The switch inside her was palpable. The sensation changed from pushing up against a soft barricade to feeling pulled in deeper and deeper, without limits. Everything about this pleased him. Her trust and subsequent submission was equal to or greater than the actual act itself. But fuck, it felt so good. He was too big to fit in her pussy completely without hitting her cervix, they had learned this the hard way, with blood and bad tears. He was always mindful of damaging her even when she begged him to push her physical boundaries. This was a unique experience and he savored every second of it. He knew it felt different for her too beyond the obvious. She had described these orgasms as ethereal and tantric. And in this moment, he knew exactly what she meant. This was a far cry from their usual bestial encounters, there was still an equal amount of passion, but with an overlying sense of tranquility and calm.

He held her gently, letting her set the pace until they were moving perfectly to the beat of the drums still playing. He watched her face change from fear to acceptance then transition into bliss and allowed himself to increase his rhythm and depth in accordance with her movements. She didn't squirm or squeal, just sighed heavily, smiled and trilled a little bit. He could feel her orgasms building with his, as her sighs became moans. He picked up the vibrator off the bed, turned it to a low pulse setting and teased her with it. She reached back between her legs and held herself open, and for a brief moment, the look of fear returned. Even with her help, it did not want to fit. He mustered the last remnants of his self-control and pulled as far out of her as he dared without losing his place and slowly worked the vibrator into her pussy.

Her reaction to this next level of penetration was instantaneous. Her moans became low and guttural. She pushed herself backwards, impaling herself on his cock and the interloping object. He could feel it pulsing between the thin wall dividing her inside. His grip on her hips tightened as he felt them both reaching climax, equally overcome by the new sensation. He entered her fully and completely as they came and cried out in unison. The pleasure was overwhelming crashing through him in waves.

She collapsed under him and it took everything he had not to do the same.

He knew from experience that aftercare was essential in this moment and shook his head to clear it a bit. She was somewhat lucid and frozen in position, scared to move. He disengaged ever so gently, sending another set of shockwaves through the both of them. As much as he wanted to fall on top of her, he knew she needed him awake and aware for one more minute. He reached into the drawer of the nightstand and pulled out a towel.

"Can you move princess?"

"Mmmmhmmm." She lifted herself up enough that he could get his arm around her waist and handed her the towel once she was upright, she tucked it quickly between her legs. He swept the pillow and toys off the bed and guided her gently into a fetal position, pulled the blankets over them and tucked himself around her. Everything else could wait, right now she needed to be held.

"That's my good girl. Are you alright?" steadying himself for whatever her reaction might be.

After a long pause, she took a deep breath, "oh my god, yes Wolfy, that was amazing." She braided her fingers into his and pulled him closer. "Except now I think I need a bath, and a nap, not necessarily in that order."

He smiled and kissed her shoulder. "Whenever you are ready princess."

"5 more minutes please."

He pulled her close in the wreck of the bed and they both drifted off to sleep.

# WITCH 

As the temperature had reached its peak midafternoon, she had given up on working for the day. The oppressive heat had exacerbated her restlessness and she found herself completely unable to focus. She silently prayed for a hint of a breeze and none came. She hated the idea of shutting the windows and turning on the a/c, to her it tasted and felt like recycled canned air, she had never cared for it. Instead she stripped down to panties and a t shirt and turned on the ceiling fan, the movement of the air helped a little. She tried to read, that wasn't working, turned the tv on and off a dozen times, she really hated television. Netflix and Pornhub were great, but not today, she wasn't in the mood for anything. She made herself a snack and sat on the patio and instead of eating had drifted in and out of daydreams. Some fantasy, like what she wanted him to do with her when he got home and others just pleasant memories of their last year together.

She recalled the first trip they had ever taken. He had sequestered them in a beautiful hotel in the middle of the woods and finally revealed his true nature. Every minute from the drive, to roaming out of the room to hunt for food, to the incredible nights naked, sipping whiskey together between ravagings had been absolute perfection. At the end of it, she had accidentally slipped into subspace in the airport and was sitting on the floor in a relatively short dress, attempting to get her boots laced up after awkwardly getting through security. With slight horror she realized anyone looking could see up her dress, and everyone was always looking at them. She looked up at him and stammered an apology. He simply said, "I know Princess, that's why I am standing here, blocking the view and protecting what is mine." Had they not had a plane to catch she would have melted into a puddle on the spot.

Quite the opposite to how she was feeling right now. Most days she could maintain some semblance of composure when they were apart, she had a thousand ways to fill the time. Not today. Restless, mind wandering, little flashes of frustration from him. She consoled herself with the fact that she had really gotten a fairly substantial bit of writing done even with the heat of the day and the continuing compulsion to pace around. She'd showered twice. Tidied the entire apartment killed a half an hour, it wasn't that big nor ever *that* messy. She'd sat down, written some more. Gotten back up, watered a thousand plants, made new playlists, answered emails and still managed to flesh out an entire chapter and start 2 more. She had thought about making something for supper, but she wasn't *that* kind of hungry. Besides, it was too hot to cook, and whatever she put on the stove before he walked in the door inevitably ended up getting burned anyways.

Even though the hours seemed to stretch into days, she had managed to distract herself long enough. 'Finally,' she thought, upon noticing the sun was starting to set. The pink sky bringing her a renewed sense of energy and excitement. She reached for him and found him frustrated but happy to be returning after a long day.

'Daddy will be home soon. Thank fuck'.

She referred to him by many things, very rarely his given name.
Calling a man 5 years her junior Daddy seemed ridiculous on paper but perfectly natural in real life, with him. They were perfectly symbiotic. The dynamic between them had made itself evident the minute they met. She knew she wanted him before he even spoke. He said the first time he looked at her all he could think to call her was "mine".

After a brief separation, they had come back together, and she had finally figured out what she was.
His.

She belonged to him. As simple as that.

She didn't identify as a 'little' exactly. She wrestled with and eventually reconciled the vernacular and stigma that came with having 'those' tendencies. She'd scoured the internet looking for something akin to how she felt when she was with him. Some of it she related to and some of it she

discarded immediately. She discovered she was both an alpha submissive and a 'middle'. She was an adult.
What he had awoken in her was a love for submitting specifically to him because he gave her a safe place to do so. She felt secure and cared for by someone she adored and respected beyond measure. She saw him as an equal, not a tyrant. The nicknames she chose denoted varying levels of playfulness, submission and reverent respect. The feeling of being with him was more like how she had felt when she was a teenager just coming into her sexuality, everything new and exciting and ripe for exploring. It was glorious.

He was the masculine to her feminine and the relationship between them was about as perfect as anything ever had been.

She had come into her happiness much later in life. And while she was grateful she had finally found him, and equally importantly herself, she sometimes cursed a universe that had kept them apart into their 40's. Righteous princess pout.

The rest of it came easily. She was fae, a good witch, a healer and a demon tamer. She lavished all her love and magic on him and in return he protected her, inspired her and sated her in ways she had only dreamed of.

She had found her love and her career at the same time. Not surprising really, just like everything else with the two of them, it had happened quite naturally. Technically it was he who had found her, sequestered in a forgotten corner of the world, and gave her the strength and will to escape her chosen perdition. He had read her writing in an attempt to learn more about her and had subsequently encouraged her beyond measure. Then he had given her plenty to write about. She now penned erotic fiction for a living. Perfect job for an introverted succubus sorceress.

One of the downfalls of this, the only one really, was the measure of good erotica is whether or not the reader becomes aroused during the story. The same was true for the writer. The more she wrote, the more turned on she became, and she had been writing a LOT lately. Truth be told she had been craving him since the minute she heard the lock click in the door as he went off to work. She enjoyed her time alone. It was necessary. But today was different.

Her entire day had been an exercise in self-discipline and patience; and she was out of patience. She took another look around the main room to reassure everything was in order and sequestered herself in the playroom. She pulled some lacy pretty things out of the trunk, undressed and redressed herself for him and settled in to wait with two of her favorite toys. Not trying to make herself cum exactly, she wanted to get caught warming herself up for when he got home. She didn't hear the keys in the door, but she knew he was home, her brow furrowed a bit when she realized she had slid the bookshelf closed behind her, out of habit. But she knew he would find her.

And he did.

"Hello my Wolf". She stopped what she was doing and barely suppressed a giggle. "Welcome home."

She watched the stress of the day leave his face as he looked at her and around the room. She felt all her own worries dissipate with his. She loved her house; especially this room, it was the inner sanctum within their sanctuary. Every modification perfectly planned out and executed. They could be their most authentic selves inside these 4 walls, hidden away from the world.

"What's my princess doing with my pussy?" she felt a shock shoot through her core, she loved it when he growled in feigned anger.

"Getting ready for you." She pulled the vibrator out to validate her statement.

He came towards her and she knelt in front of him on the bed. Enjoying this part of the ritual almost as much as what came next.

If this apartment was sanctuary, and it truly was, this room was a secret temple and his body was the alter she prayed at. The first time she had ever laid eyes on him he was standing in front of her bar, unbuttoning his cuffs, the sight of him doing this every time since never failed to get her blood racing and her princess parts tingling. Her fingers trembled a little as she unbuttoned his shirt and fumbled with his belt buckle, trying to appear calm and collected when she was anything but. Her pussy was hungry for more after she'd teased herself, the princess plug urgently reminding her of its presence with every miniscule moment. She was starving and wanted to be filled, this time by him.

He pulled her to him and played with her hair. She wrapped her arms around his torso briefly, enjoying the sensation of his warm skin against the coolness of her cheek. She bowed her head and took him into her mouth. Playfully licking and teasing at first, then allowing his hands and hips to guide her. She loved the switch when his gentle caresses became commanding grasps and his breathing became low groans and bellows of pleasure. She struggled and choked the slightest bit but didn't stop until he pulled away enough to let her catch her breath.

She looked up at him. These brief moments of lucidity where she had control of all her faculties were rare. They held a close second to the crashing waves of orgasms he coaxed from her body. She looked at him, smiling down at her, knowing she looked a mess, tear filled panda eyes, black mascara running down her cheeks, spit wetting her lips, she felt slightly ruined but look on his face was nothing but adoration with the promise of something wicked. She was constantly overwhelmed by how beautiful he was and how much she loved him and how badly she wanted him inside of her, right fucking now.

Although she had orchestrated this, she still had a flash of shyness. She wasn't used to vocalizing her desires. They had a telepathic link that was even more prevalent when their bodies were joined, he always knew what she needed, she rarely had to use her words. He was being patient and playful. She knew she wouldn't get what she wanted unless she said it out loud, but she still couldn't summon the words. She dropped her eyes and he immediately grabbed her chin and made her meet his gaze sending a lightning bolt of fresh lust through her core. He broke the silence, asking her what she wanted.

Everywhere, other than naked in front of him, she was poised and incredibly articulate. But not here and not now. "I want...I want... I want you to fuck me in the ass." She heard herself stutter in a whisper. "Please."

He grinned a wicked grin and took control back from her.

She sighed with relief and positioned herself as he requested. Face down on the bed, arching her back as much as she could, and then a little bit more for good measure. She could imagine what she looked like in that moment, ass cheeks framed in lace, pussy glistening and still swollen from the night before. Bejeweled butt plug catching the light. She was contemplating asking him to turn on the video camera when she felt the tip of his cock parting her lips. She was taken by surprise, first by him and second by how quickly she climaxed. She hadn't allowed herself to cum before he got home and was more worked up than she realized it seemed. He teased her by being gentle and following the tempo of the drums playing in the background.

The glorious feeling of fireworks radiated out from her core and her pussy twitched around his massive cock. She heard him telling her to cum, her body needed no further encouragement, she heard herself babble something incoherent and then the sensation of falling. She lost consciousness for the briefest of moments, grateful for the pillow holding her up. The feeling of being completely full was overwhelming at best.

"Is that what you wanted my love?"

She hadn't fully recovered from her orgasm and answered honestly but flippantly. The truth was, yes. She always wanted him. Every minute of every day in every way.

A solid, loud slap on her ass brought her back to reality. She snapped back to attention and immediately remembered what she had asked for and why they were here. Yet another dilemma, even in her brattiest moments, the word 'no' got stuck in her throat, she didn't like saying it to him on a good day, much less bent over in front of him on the heels of an amazing orgasm.

She watched him raise his hand again and she answered quickly and quietly. "Yes and no", steadying herself for another smack if he was not pleased with her answer and instead being rewarded with soft caresses on her stinging flesh. She found her brave and pushed it a little further, removing the tiny plug was a tease, she wanted him inside of her so very badly. She held herself open and said "Now you. Please."

He took care of her always, even in his roughest moments when he was ravaging her as a beast it was with preparation. She quivered in anticipation, temporarily lost in the sensation of being massaged firmly and thoroughly with an overabundance of lubrication. She knew there would be pain, just as she knew it wouldn't last and the calmer and more relaxed she could keep herself, the sooner the pleasure would come. She rested her full body weight onto the pillow feeling slightly betrayed by her own body as it twitched every time he hit that particular spot. She was rather afraid; he was huge, and this was not something they did often enough for it to become routine or easy. But she had a craving, and she wanted to please him. It felt as though every nerve ending had gathered in the space between her legs and was on high alert. He teased her with fingers just inside her pussy, driving her mad.

"It's okay baby, I won't hurt you." His voice was kind and reassuring. She believed him and moreover she trusted him. With this promise her mind finally won over matter and she felt herself quiet enough to accept what was coming. He was good to his word and didn't push too much or too quickly.

She had properly prepared herself somewhat for this, so the pain passed almost immediately, turning to a dull ache as she fought to remain still and to not tense up and fight what was happening. She concentrated on the heat from his hands touching her skin, the sound of the drums, reminiscent of a heartbeat and then bliss.

Her skin began to tingle, as if she was connected to some low voltage current lazily surging though every part of her. This was not anything like her other orgasms, this was a slow build into ecstasy. She had heard those who tried heroin describe a very similar feeling of sensory disconnection but with a hyper awareness of every tingling cell in her body. Like the thrum of pins and needles but everywhere all at once and without the hurt. Her orgasms didn't build and crash, just overlapped lazily and she let them. Caught up in the sound of the drums, the electricity coursing through her and the feeling of being filled by him over and over, deeper and impossibly deeper with every stroke.

She heard a faint buzzing and felt a pulse touching her pussy, she flinched with fear momentarily, then reached back and tried to open herself to no avail. She was not able to move are speak or do much of anything other than just enjoy the beautifully bizarre sensations her body was experiencing. Then suddenly sensory overload. She felt full to the breaking point, multiple orgasms rippling and crashing over top of each other and straight through her. She breached and collapsed as a familiar feeling of floating engulfed her. Completely submerged in subspace.

She had no idea how long she had been gone. She felt him tenderly removing the vibrator from her throbbing pussy with a wet gush. Her body tensed slightly as he slowly slid his cock out of her. Nerve racking even though she was still coming in and out of awareness. She heard him ask if she could move and allowed herself to be placed into a less vulnerable position. The towel felt rough and foreign between her legs, but she knew she was a mess and at least this would keep it contained until she could move, maybe a week from now, if she was lucky. Her skin was hyper-sensitive, and her muscles had no intention of cooperating or moving much at all.

He called her his good girl and she couldn't help but swoon just a little bit. She was so grateful for this man of hers. Every fucked-up fantasy she had ever had, every bit of porn she could never admit to watching he took not just in stride but recreated with enthusiasm. The way he was holding her now, like she was some kind of precious thing and not a dirty little fuck doll that had just taken a monster cock in her ass and then some.

She realized he had asked if she was alright, and she hadn't answered.

"Oh my god, yes Wolfy, that was amazing." She tucked herself into him and managed to mumble something hopefully coherent about needing a bath before sleep took her.

## Can't wait to see what comes next for the Witch and her Wolfy? Check out this teaser:

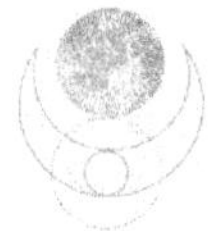

*She had always been strange.*

*There was no denying that fact anymore, not that she wanted to. It was exhausting pretending to be what she wasn't. And with him she didn't have to hide a thing.*

*As the years passed, she learned very slowly to embrace the ostracism and fear from the humans so prevalent on this plane, then all at once. She knew if she had been born in any other century, she would have been either exalted as an oracle or burned at the stake. She had a feeling she had been both. Memories presenting as dreams of other lifetimes, fighting monsters, healing, advising. Visions of drowning, burning and even in this life anything around her neck still felt like a hangman's noose.*

*Except his hand.*

*That felt like safety, submission and home.*

*She had not known exactly what he was when he found her, not right away. Only recognized a creature of the dark struggling to exist in the light. Pulled towards her by the Stella Polaris in her chest that only those carrying their own magic could see. He wasn't the first to have sought her out. There was something in him hidden, denied and caged.*

*She felt it coming off him in waves blood pulsing in Morse code as her fingertips touched his skin. She wanted to touch him so badly it became a compulsion. She heard the familiar words that seemed to always flow from stranger's mouths upon meeting her, seeing her. Exclaiming "I can't believe I am telling you this" with alarming regularity the night they met.*
*She simply smiled reassuringly, rested her hand on his knee and let him purge all of the angst he had been carrying around.*

Will this be the lifetime they fulfill their karmic destiny or are they so consumed with desire for each other that history has no choice but to repeat itself...

# STAY TUNED.

www.ingramcontent.com/pod-product-compliance
Lightning Source LLC
Chambersburg PA
CBHW061433050726
47593CB00006B/2339